# DARLING OR DEVIL ?

## A GIRL WITH A FIGHTER MIND

PRACHI PATIL

Copyright © Prachi Patil
All Rights Reserved.

ISBN 978-1-68554-072-2

This book has been published with all efforts taken to make the material error-free after the consent of the author. However, the author and the publisher do not assume and hereby disclaim any liability to any party for any loss, damage, or disruption caused by errors or omissions, whether such errors or omissions result from negligence, accident, or any other cause.

While every effort has been made to avoid any mistake or omission, this publication is being sold on the condition and understanding that neither the author nor the publishers or printers would be liable in any manner to any person by reason of any mistake or omission in this publication or for any action taken or omitted to be taken or advice rendered or accepted on the basis of this work. For any defect in printing or binding the publishers will be liable only to replace the defective copy by another copy of this work then available.

*This book is dedicated to my friend :*

## MISS. GAURI NITIN WAGHOLIKAR

# Contents

| | |
|---|---|
| *Reach* | *vii* |
| *Mystery* | *ix* |
| *Darling Or Devil ?* | *xi* |
| *The Ordeal Of Every Person* | *xiii* |
| *Preface* | *xv* |
| *Acknowledgements* | *xvii* |
| *Prologue* | *xix* |
| 1. Begain | 1 |
| 2. Her Parents Struggle | 3 |
| 3. The Great Joy Of Her Life | 5 |
| 4. A Few Days Later: | 6 |
| 5. Her Outside World | 8 |
| 6. Painful Journey | 10 |
| 7. When Life Turns Back | 13 |
| 8. Happiness | 16 |
| 9. How She Built Herself | 19 |
| 10. The Life Of Lockdown | 21 |
| 11. A Painful Part | 26 |
| 12. Yes, I Came In Her Life | 30 |
| 13. Still Running Struggle | 32 |
| Some Points | 33 |

# Reach

*To reach at me :-*

*patilprachu111@gmail.com*

# Mystery

*"Mere har samasya ka karan bhi mai,*
*Mere har samasya ka nivaran bhi mai"*

# Darling Or Devil ?

*In this book*
  *Darling means:-*

*Darling means she is excellent in someone's mortal. It is so good that she blindly trust the person in front of her. And this darlingness ruined her one day.*

*Devil means:-*

*Devil means if someone ridicules her, she becomes a Devil. If the person in front does wrong with the cuckold then she forgets her darlingness and becomes a devil.*

# The Ordeal Of Every Person

*"Incarnate god or human*
*all are made of it*
*be the king or the subjects*
*become a slave to all circumstances*


*First Lanka than in a forest*
*Sita cries sitting*
*litmus test on the path of life*
*everyone has to give*
*Treta, Dwapara or Kali Yuga*
*no one has survived*
*This ordeal for centuries*
*man has given*


*Radha teaches love*
*distance from Kanha*
*litmus test on the path of life*
*everyone has to give*


*your life is precious*
*But fleeting is this physique*
*pain, pleasure or hate, desire*
*the living body has an illusion*
*Yashodhara as wife*
*far from buddha*
*litmus test on the path of life*
*everyone has to give*

## THE ORDEAL OF EVERY PERSON

*the quality of speech*
*do everything with patience*
*Karma is the only god worship*
*name it life*


*In precious moments of happiness and sorrow*
*eyes are moist*
*litmus test on the path of life*
*everyone has to give*
*And in the same way, Gauri also had to pass some ordeal"*

# Preface

In every chapter of this book, you will get to see darling or the devil And frequently people ask Gauri what have you achieved?

Life is all about struggle. In this book that girl continuously strives for happiness in her life.
Happiness is the real motive for which she struggles in her life.
But for that she has to fight, she has to endure the pain, the hardships.
And not only that she has to struggle with herself also because if she can conquer herself, then she can be victorious in any front of her life.....
As She always said that:-

**"Mere har samasya ka karan bhi mai,
Aur mere har samasya ka nivaran bhi mai"**

She gave the key to unlocking the treasure of happiness which she seeks for
her whole lives.

"In my book, I discuss my friend her experience and how she fought her life, and how she built herself, how she becomes a successful guy

*you will find stories and mentors that
I hope will touch your heart"*

# Acknowledgements

Well, to say this is my book would be accurate based on my friend Gauri's life story.
It's my good luck that I'm writing her novel.

I would like to express my special thanks of gratitude to my friend as well as my sister

**"Miss Gauri wagholikar"** for their able guidance and assistance in completing my book. Also, thank you to give me this opportunity to compose your novel.

I would also like to extend my appreciation to my mother **"Mrs. Anita Patil"** for provisioning me with all the comfort that was needed.

DATE:- 28-08-2021.

PRACHI-PATIL

# Prologue

*Start Where You are is an interactive journal designed to help readers nurture their creativity, mindfulness, and self-motivation.*

*It helps readers navigate the confusion and chaos of daily life with a simple reminder: that by taking the time to know ourselves and what those dreams are, we can appreciate the world around us and achieve our dreams.*

*Featuring vibrant hand-lettering and images that have attracted a large following for her stationery and textile line in boutiques across the country, Prachi Patil's uplifting book presents supportive prompts and exercises along with inspirational quotes to encourage reflection through writing, drawing, chart-making, and more.*

*Featuring inspiring quotes from writers, artists, and other visionaries paired with open-ended questions and prompts, with plenty of room for writing and reflecting, this appealing full-color book will make a perfect gift and keepsake as well as being a powerful tool for positive change.*

## CHAPTER I
# Begain

*This story initiates by Shahpur,*

*A well-known small village in India. Once upon a time, a soul was to be born on earth, maybe she was that soul.*

*Everyone was anxiously waiting for the baby to be born in wagholikar's family. The awesome ritual will begin in the house to gonna arrive.*

*There was happiness in the house and many beautiful presents came from relatives and friends. The child's parents were delighted to arrive at the baby.*

*A baby girl has been born on 16 September 1999, in shahpur city, Maharastra. A calm baby girl whose face was glowing with light, delight, and marvelous mystery, There was an ambiance of happiness in the house of the arrival of a baby girl, Everyone was wondering by what name to call this little angel.*

*Extremely charmingly that little angel was named Gauri by her father, Ganpati Bappa had come at that time and she was the 1$^{st}$ child in her house,*

*Now that little angel will be called by the name Gauri. It was as if happiness had come of Gauri's arrival. her parents were also going through a struggle period.*

## CHAPTER II

# Her Parents Struggle

*After 3 months :-*

*Her parents were working very hard to provide a good life for their daughter.*

*Her mother is a teacher and she wanted to join her school. And afterward, Gauri was a little girl. her mother struggled a lot, She would do all the household chores, after that she would be ready to go to school, and Her daughter was in the creche while she worked.*

*Gauri's father was also busy with their work because Struggle time was going on for her father too, he used to be very busy.*

*When her dad goes to an office in the morning, she was asleep and her dad has come she was sleeping because her father exploited to be late in coming home from the office.*

*Her father had a holiday on Thursday, so her father plays with her all day and clicks photos of her, One day so many photos were clicked that the camera role was over. Her father likes her a lot, she is her daddy's little princess.*

*Her mother loves her daughter more than herself.*

*Her grannie was her best friend from childhood.*

CHAPTER III

# The great joy of her life

*Time promulgated and another new happiness was to come in the wagholikar's house*

*On July 19, 2003, Gauri's younger brother arrived,*

*Gauri was so happy because she got a partner, a new best friend, and another soul of her. that little boy was named Abhishek, she plays with him a lot.*

*They were both like the best buddies. they may play together and live very well, Wherever they go, they may go together, Both of them used to go to take May together till Chochlaate, even if they wanted to go down from the house, they used to go together. Everyone used to see them and speak, wherever they are seen, they are seen together. They both share their secret with each other, That girl never needed a friend, her brother was everything to her,*

## CHAPTER IV

# A few days later:

**A few days later:**

Gauri started to understand everything, and she started taking care of her brother, absence of her Parents, They both play together, study together.

one day:

It was the day of Rang Panchami, she and her mother and her brother, they used to fill water in colorful balloons, In the evening after her father comes from office, And standing by the roof, they used to throw balls of ballons at her father.

How our little angel Gauri grew up did not know the time. See when did the girl grow up.

Now Gauri has come in $12^{th}$. The subject was PCMB and She has very good at studies.

*Traveling far away from home, then she just travels and goes to class and studies after eyesight everything in the house. With all these struggles, she passes out 12th standard with 1st class. At home, her parents never obligatory her for marks.*

*Her parents and her brother congratulated her for passes out 12 standards.*

*Her parents was the commencement to proud of her, Now her bustling with prospect arrangement ahead.*

*She took the admission for engineering at* **All India Shri Shivaji Memorial Society Institute Of Information Technology.**

## CHAPTER V

# Her outside world

*She was a simple girl, she may not know about the outside world, And she may have made the first move as a teenager, her college had started, her life was passing enjoyment and cavort, everyone's feet slip in teenagers, the same thing happened with her, her foot slipped too.*

*New friends outsider world she got it all together and her foot slipped.*

*In all this she earned some friends, Their names are Yash, Anuj, Anjali, and Kshitiya. And this is her best friends, Whose friendship she never doubted, That friend who not ever moving out her side in a confounded world full of pots, And now she might ascertain the exterior world.*

*Friends and the exterior atmosphere had come under the leverage of adolescence, her feet started gliding.*

*Her pride was gradually passing away from her studies, Now her evil mood was being seen in the home too.*

*Her parents were thinking about what to do with this girl, her parents explained to her many times, but she would understand at that time and later she exploited to contemplate the exterior atmosphere as I possess, Her existence two lives commencement life was subsistence life with fun and secondary life, that girl with an examination, results and parent's reaction to them, Brokenhearted after being a failure in commencement life, And if there is a failure in secondary life, life sounds like to be pointless, How does it feel when the huge nightmare is wiped out?*

*Gauri also proverb, something similar, She was apprehensive that she would break down in the examination Because she knew that she has watched the aggregate annual exclusively for the enjoyment and the exterior world.*

*Gauri's examination nearly and she gave the papers, her parents asked for it how the examination went she said that my examination is going perfectly.*

CHAPTER VI

# Painful Journey

*The vacation was a seldom day subsequently the examination, The result date was also approaching. one day her mumma's birthday, Everyone was celebrating her Mumma's birthday at home.*

*How did fortune play with that girl? Her result was displayed on the same day, Her friend Yash call her and tell about the result, she failed in exams, her first year was down, She was shocked to hear all that.*

*The happy atmosphere at home, She was thinking so how can I tell, Still she thought that I will not hide anything from anyone, I will have to tell the truth, gathered a lot of courage that she told everyone, she said I have failed, my year is down. The whole family was shocked to hear all this, her parents were thinking about her, her parents were not talking to her, she was grumbling inside, recalling everything, She has not failed till that girl, the one who got the best grade in the house, failed today.*

*Her father felt that now she is not able to do engineering and they want to get her admission to BCA course, her parents went to college to get canceling her admission, and departed to the principal's office, principal sir endeavored a lot to comprehend her parents, Patil sir also straightened out to her parents, couldn't revoke her admission, Her parents also decided, to give her a opportunity, Her father did not speak to her for 1 month, everyone got a huge collision, she was disappointed inside, she just sat quietly, but her mother to take her outside, Be her best friend that her mother supported her at that time, her mother was able to see her every pain, knows all your pain , mother knows you more than you*
*How long will you hide yourself from your mother mom knows everthing,*


*Subsequently one month her father came to her and asked what to do next, she said "**I want to persevere my study**", Her father aforementioned, all right to get out all the subjects at at one time, she sat down to studies but Maybe her economic crisis was consumption her from the imprisoned,*

*She secondhand to assemble in one site for hours just thinking, at that time neither of her friends came to her, even no one called her, she had a lot of friends, and she had a lot of attachment with those friends, But if she finds friends who support her on time, then just 2-4.*

*The rest may leave her with her tough time, Friends whose tough time Gauri helped by leaving her own work, Maybe she was starting to realize now, except the family members, no one supports.*

*she was crying alone on a side of her room's corner, The first failure of her life The reality which she is considering as a beautiful dream is a nightmare.*

*What she thought of as freedom had become a life sentence for her.*

*She stuck around depressed in the manner of this for one year.*

## CHAPTER VII
# When life turns back

Then the day came in which she had to go to college How will she go to college, how will she keep up with the juniors she used to flaunt?And because of her frustration, she didn't even go out of the house. Her brother also a fear about her,

**One day :**

Her voice came from imprisoned and she told herself to get up and do something and subsequently she set out for her own struggle. Failure was an opportunity for her that life had given her to make her better than before.

she had given up on this small failure of her. She fought with failure and fought eyes with failure and she said, but now I will not lose dearly,no matter what happens, I will fall and fight again, she took this failure as a lesson, and i will learn everything from that lesson, "If I fail today, I will get success tomorrow", Failure is the start of her success story.

*She decided that now she will bring back her self-confidence, "Closing Your Eyes Doesn't Eliminate Danger" and she felt it. She started working hard to study day and night She read each chapter carefully, understand every topic, Although a little depressed she was still there she devoted her full attention to her studies, she took the help of her teachers, Teachers also fully supported to her, those nights she cries, and thought my parents because of my mistakes bowed his head down after a lot of hard work, One day her father came to her and said to her, you try to do hard work I am with you. His father helped her a lot, That day she got some courage.*

*In all this her mother supported her a lot. Her mother asked her I have been watching for a long time, you are looking troubled, what happened dear, Just hearing that her eyes were moist, Maybe she realized that no one understood her at this bad time, But mumma understood without knowing, her mumma asked her what happened dear tell me, Her mother says dear don't panic I am with you, Hearing this, she started getting courage,*

*"Her childhood's blank paper decoration is her mother, the secret formula of her success is her mother, her uncle chips are her mother Wherever she go today, people praise you a lot, The girl is intelligent, cultured & all But only the potter gives shape to a clay. she was nothing, it is her mother who*

*made her she have every good in her, This thought her is because of them. The values given by her mom are her foundation. Her manners are in her nature because of them. This view of her, which tests right and wrong, is the view given by her mother".*

## After 2-3 days:

*Finally the days of exams have come, she gave exams, her papers went well, hardwork that was done,*

CHAPTER VIII

# Happiness

*Her result displayed, and it's a pleasure, she did it, she cleared all the subjects all at once, her parents was very happy, Her brother wish her congratulations and was very happy,*

Gauri understood now what was right and wrong for her. She used to put limits on herself, And now he was slowly understanding, If her parents had not told her that 1 month, she would not have been here today.

She never misunderstood her parents, always respect, but just for some time her foot slipped, And her parents also treated her well, that's why today she has become capable of this. All relatives were congratulating her.

If the pressure is high, then it burns to ashes, if it is less then everything dries up, but if the flame is right then this heat makes something beautiful her parents knew this very well, And that's what made her so high today, she understood that if her parents had kept her, then it was good for her,

Her parents know By giving too much relaxation, children get spoiled and by keeping too much limit, *children become disheartened, they start suppressing their words inside, she has learned everything by watching the struggle of her parents. Gauri wants to speak to her parents through this book :*

**"Dear mom and dad thank you so much for giving me this life, you both have done a lot for me, thank you for supporting me in my hard times. I love you aai baba."**

**Gauri also want to speak to her mumma:** *"Truth be told, life is not easy to get,The one who gave me life, she is my mother, When I saw her for the first time, her face blossomed, that she had tears in her eyes and she had got a daughter in my form, When I laugh she laughs When I cry she cries, I was so stupid I even know what is mother, Neither the morsel was picked up by hand nor did it go away on its own. It was very easy for me to cry but her hand used to come forward to wipe away the tears. When I grew up a little, I felt that there are many relationships too but every relationship happens only after the mother, When I was alive alone, I remembered her, when it was dark, I remembered her, How easy it takes to think this life, but when I started living I remembered her, Now mumma, I tell you one thing after that don't tell me anything, you are my life, you stay with me at every turn, I love you mumma"*

Has Gauri achieved everything?

*Is Gauri's struggle over now?*

## CHAPTER IX
# How she built herself

*Gauri was all clear now,*

*But*

she had the impel to make her label. then what was she decided, now if she wants to make herself, then she will have to do it.

Now she wanted to build herself, wanted to be mentally strong, she set her goal, she put limits on herself for everything, continued her studies, studied hard and diligently, took care of the house.

She had won back the trust of her parents, she started thinking positive, she dare to shut out all the distractions, dare to shut out the world,

*She updated her studies, And at the same time she started teaching outside, She used to go to class to learn some programming language,she got an offer from her, you teach programming to our children. but she rejected that offer, because she just had to focus on herself,*

*Time passed slowly*

CHAPTER X

# The life of Lockdown

Corona epidemic had obtained in our motherland, The government had handed down, constraining all over, All colleges and schools were locked,

Everybody was incarcerated in the house for 2-3 months, Exterior circumstances was very bad due to corona,

Many people were anxious because of this ailment.

That girl thought that something new should be done in it.

she thought why not me these free days I should learn housework, And that girl learned many things in those days, she had a lot of talent too.

Every year with the emergence of Bappa, the idol of Bappa is made by Gauri,

*Let's see how the idol is made by her in the last year.*

*How beautiful it is,*

she has a lot of talent, but some people just couldn't see her talent. and many more creative minds, She sees everything practically.

Now, due to Lockdown, all the sources were almost online even for studies. So, she thought of giving flight to her future in this too, from her programming skills applied for Internships from Internshala, And as we know how smart she is, she got internships. And one day came where she rejected many internships and jobs Because she had to give a good flight to her future.

Her philosophy was such that it is superior to be sad in someone's heartache than to live in today, appreciate his work so that he comes out of tension and problems, Go take that in his misery or sorrow or misery increases, her spirits were acquiring strengthened with time. That girl is not one of those who rely on time, she knows **"Intelligence may fail but the effort will not"**.

She loves to write poetry,

She had a lot of talent hidden in her.

Let's see some examples of her talents

*she has a hobby of writing above today by thinking on her own.*

*Just recently came Shershaah movie, she saw that movie and wrote something on it.*

*Let's see what she wrote*

"बचपन से उसने बस एक सपना देखा था
फौजी बनके लढना जैसे उसने आखों पे बंधा था
हरा पीला कहा पसंद उसको लाल खून से इश्क था
भारत माँ का शेरे वो हर वक़्त लढाई लढता था
दोस्तो में जान रहकर दलि कही और था
उस शेरनी ने भी उनका प्यार संभाला भी क्या खूब था
सीमा पे न हारा वो एक शेरनी से दलि हारा था
पर उन दोनो ने अपना प्यार भारत माँ को सोपा था
सेना में जवान और हुनर का ये पक्का था
उमर बस २३ साल पर शेरे जैसे दहाडता था
जजबा उसके खून में और जीत का लगाम हाथ था
शेरेशाहा से जवाजा गया ये जवान तगडा फौजी था
अपनो के लिए प्यार और दुश्मन के लिए तलवार था
कम उमर में भी इनका रवैया कुछ अलग ही था
कैप्टन विक्रम बत्रा जैसे हिंदुस्तान शान था
लडता रहा अंत तक न हार मानी थी
लढा था वो इसे जैसे काश्मीर उसकी शान थी
अपनी जान की बाजी लगाये जीत हासलि हुए थी
अंत की वो जंग नकिली गोली सनिसे लगा ली
दुश्मन से न रुका वो लालडा भारत में समा गया
इस एक जीत ने सबकी आंखों को नम कयिा

मां बाप को गर्व और प्रयितमा की सूनी थी कलाई
चारो तरफ थी तबाही और गगनसे भी शोर हुआ
पर साहब कहा माने उनका दलि मांग रहा मोर था"

*what a wonderful and wonderful write up, Such is the art of her.*

## CHAPTER XI

# A painful part

Due to corona, the corona was happening in everyone's house, everyone was worried about this epidemic.

On the other hand, Gauri's father got corona in his family too, he was shifted to the hospital.

Gauri's mother and her brother also got the report of Corona positive, if both of them existed in the house, now the girl was assumed all responsibility, took care of part two of the hospital, and took care of all the house too.

At that time the situation was such that even the relatives could not come.

Her father was thinking inside: -

"White walls all around
Green sheet in place of ground

*A single-pole instead of three*
*Tied on a bed instead of free*
*Drip in place of gloves*
*And glucose in place of loaves*
*Holding millions of dreams*
*Laying in hospital with screens*
*Life is waiting ahead*
*While I am tied on bed*
*Holding the scissors of hope*
*To cut down the unseen rope*
*Playing with the tube of DNS bottle*
*At age of playing home and hotel*
*To conclude the pain*
*I have a lot to gain*
*I'll rise above restlessness*
*To beat the demon of helplessness*
*All the pain is temporary*
*Since I have two little children and one beautiful wife"*.


She did not give up, her father's condition was critical, She was very scared to see her father's critical condition, But she could not cry because she had to take care of everything, she cries alone at night after coming home,

and she thinks:

"bitter gourd from above
sweet inside
papa with you
happily touches the sky


Putting it under the ear hard on the mistake...
Scolding yourself inside.
And after a few moments with bad jokes
make me cry myself,


no matter how much I try to hide, I can't hide my pain.
sit close and speak, I am your sympathizer, showing
eyes, drinking water without a brush, And when the
fever comes, by putting a stopper first,
then give medicine papa like you
Why not travel this world


I went to tell you about The ocean of alphabets was
formed. Just now, I was a child I don't know when I
grew up".


and she cries the whole night,


she was worried about her mother's health


After some days:

*Finally her father's health was getting better.*

*At that time she used to pray every day, God takes my life but keep my parents safe, Being the eldest daughter of the house, she used to see everything, And she did her responsibilities very well. She handled everything so well,*

*Her Mumma papa feels very proud of her, And feel proud why not, Where are such children in today's world? Her parents feel very proud of her.*

## CHAPTER XII

# Yes, I came in her life

*I saw you Gauri didi first time near the playground of our college, I meet her for the first time in the month of July but she doesn't see me. she are so cool after some time she saves my mobile number but the reason is the cricket team, that's why she save my number she was so much different than other girls that day is special for me, I want to talk with her but can't gather the courage to speak with her, I tried to talk to her, but she was busy with friends,*

*After that exams happened lockdown happened*

*I saw you Gauri didi first time near the playground of our college, I meet her for the first time in the month of July but she doesn't see me. she are so cool after some time she saves my mobile number but the reason is the cricket team, that's why she save my number she was so much different than other girls that day is special for me, I want to talk with her but can't gather the courage to speak with her, I tried to talk to her, but she was busy with friends,*
*After that exams happened lockdown happened*
*looking forward to speak with her*
*and they talk with each other about what's up for some reason, that days her father condition was critical due to corona and I ask every day her, how is your father, about their condition she tells me and she*

*felt free to talk with me their bonding getting strong day by day I was so happy, because no one in the house used to speak to her with love and that days I was waiting to someone true friend to understand my feeling and finally I got my true friend Gauri,*
*looking forward to meet with her*
*and I get a green signal*
*i contact her instantly*
*she recieve the call and i get positive response from her*
*finally we will meet each other i was so happy I was very much excited to see her finally i reached pune and after wait of 1 hour 18 minutes she meet me and i considered gauri as my ideal guru, she helped me to get out of depression,*
*Now i have to go back to my hometown, our friendship bond was very strong, but a few days later, she suddenly stopped talking to me, I thought maybe I did something wrong, Later I came to know that she have not give time their own problems, And my mistakes are too many, so because of that they have stopped talking to me. Maybe now I have become a devil part in her life,*
*I had to say sorry to you that's why I couldn't find a better way*
*" forgive me i have denied again and again, that i have done wrong, my words and my actions i can not justify, all the sorrow I put you through, all the tears you have cried , I am sorry may not be enough to pick up the broken pieces, forgive me for the damage I have caused and for my stupid ways, you're such a good person and i am just someone who ruined your days, I am so sorry for everything ".*

## CHAPTER XIII
# Still running struggle

*She's still finding the love of her life who can understand her in her way and take care of her like a little baby. but on the other hand she's fighting with the problems and getting back on a track.*

# Some Points

- *"Mere har samasya ka karan bhi mai,*

  *Mere har samasya ka nivaran bhi mai"*

- Life is all about struggle.

- Be your own light.

- Adjustment is a very important thought every moment in our life because it gives mainly peace, understanding, and love between any matter.

- On self-confidence: "Our doubts are traitors and cause us to miss the good we oft might win, by fearing to attempt."

www.ingramcontent.com/pod-product-compliance
Lightning Source LLC
LaVergne TN
LVHW021738060526
838200LV00052B/3339